A NOTE TO PARENTS

Disney's First Readers Level 2 books were created for beginning readers who are gaining confidence in their early reading skills.

Compared to Level 1 books, **Level 2** books have slightly smaller type and contain more words to a page. Although sentence structure is still simple, the stories are slightly longer and more complex.

Just as children need training wheels when learning to ride a bicycle, they need the support of a good model when learning to read. Every time your child sees that you enjoy reading, whether alone or with him or her, you provide the encouragement needed to build reading confidence. Here are some helpful hints to use with the **Disney's First Readers Level 2** books:

★ Play or act out each character's words. Change your voice to indicate which character is speaking. As your child becomes comfortable with the printed text, he or she can take a favorite character's part and read those passages.

★ Have your child try reading the story. If your child asks about a word, do not interrupt the flow of reading to make him or her sound it out. Pronounce the word for your child. If, however, he or she begins to sound it out, be gently encouraging—your child is developing phonetic skills!

★ Read aloud. It's still important at this level to read to your child. With your child watching, move a finger smoothly along the text. Do not stop at each word. Change the tone of your voice to indicate punctuation marks, such as questions and exclamations. Your child will begin to notice how words and punctuation marks make sense and can make reading fun.

★ Let your child ask you questions about the story. This will help to develop your child's critical thinking skills. Use the After-Reading Fun activities provided at the end of each book as a fun exercise to further enhance your child's reading skills.

★ Praise all reading efforts warmly and often!

Remember that early-reading experiences that you share with your child can help him or her to become a confident and successful reader later on!

— Patricia Koppman
Past President
International Reading Association

First published by Disney Press, New York, New York.
This edition published by Scholastic Inc.,
90 Old Sherman Turnpike, Danbury, Connecticut 06816
by arrangement with Disney Licensed Publishing.

SCHOLASTIC and associated logos are trademarks of Scholastic Inc.

ISBN 0-7172-6464-5

Printed in the U.S.A.

Tarzan Goes Bananas

by Judy Katschke
Painted by Andrea and John Alvin

Disney's First Readers — Level 2
A Story from Disney's *Tarzan*

SCHOLASTIC INC.

New York Toronto London Auckland Sydney
Mexico City New Delhi Hong Kong Buenos Aires

"Have fun today, Tarzan," Kala said.
"And try to stay out of trouble."

Terk had an idea. "Let's have a banana-picking contest!"

The friends spread the word
through the jungle. Terk ran
through the trees. So did Tarzan.

WHOOPS!

Tarzan spread the word his way.
"Hey, everybody!" he shouted. "We're
having a contest!"

"Does he always have to yell?" asked Tantor.

"The rules are easy,"
Terk told the animals.
"If you pick the most
bananas, you win."

The baboon went first. He picked
some bananas. But he ate them, too!
"Peels don't count!" Terk shouted.

Tarzan got an idea.

The rhino tried. He couldn't
do it. He got stuck!
"Nice try, bud," Terk said.

The snake tried. She couldn't
do it. She had no hands!

"NEXT!" Terk shouted.

More animals tried. They couldn't do it either.

Tarzan worked on his idea to get the most bananas.

"Go for it, Tantor," Terk said.

Tantor was about to try when . . .

"EEK! A LIZARD!"

Tantor was scared. He bumped against the tree and began to shake. The tree shook, too. And down came ten bananas!

"My turn!" Terk said. Terk climbed to the top. She hung from a leaf and began to pick.

". . . thirteen . . . fourteen . . . fifteen . . ."

The stem snapped. Terk and the bananas fell down!

Tarzan had a plan.

"It's your turn, Tarzan," Terk said. Tarzan didn't climb like a baboon, slither like a snake, or knock his head like a rhino.

Ready . . . aim . . . WHACK!
"Wow!" Terk said.
"You won."

"This contest was fun," Tarzan said.

"And we stayed out of trouble!"
Tantor said.

"Or, maybe we didn't!"
Terk said.

Enhance the reading experience with follow-up questions to help your child develop reading comprehension and increase his/her awareness of words.

Approach this with a sense of play. Make a game of having your child answer the questions. You do not need to ask all the questions at one time. Let these questions be fun discussions rather than a test. If your child doesn't have instant recall, encourage him/her to look back into the book to "research" the answers. You'll be modeling what good readers do and, at the same time, forging a sharing bond with your child.

Tarzan Goes Bananas

1. What was Kala's warning to Tarzan?

2. Why do you think Terk suggested a banana-picking contest?

3. Who won the contest and how was it done?

4. What kind of contest could you win?

5. How many different kinds of fruit can you name?

6. How many words can you name that begin with "b" like banana?

Answers : 1. to stay out of trouble. 2. Terk thought that she would be good at getting bananas and that she could win. 3. Tarzan won the contest by throwing a spear that shook all the bananas out of the tree. 4. answers will vary. 5. possible answers: apples, oranges, grapes, pears, pineapples, etc. 6. possible answers: baby, bicycle, big, bird, bug, etc.